22.

To John Farman, who always gets the joke – C. C. and S. C.

FUNNY!
A HUTCHINSON BOOK 0 09 176949 3

Published in Great Britain by Hutchinson,
an imprint of Random House Children's Books

This edition published 2004

1 3 5 7 9 10 8 6 4 2

Text copyright © Caroline Castle, 2004
Illustrations copyright © Sam Childs, 2004

The right of Caroline Castle and Sam Childs to be identified as
the author and illustrator of this work has been asserted in accordance with
the Copyright, Designs and Patents Act 1988.

RANDOM HOUSE CHILDREN'S BOOKS
61–63 Uxbridge Road, London W5 5SA
A division of The Random House Group Ltd

RANDOM HOUSE AUSTRALIA (PTY) LTD
20 Alfred Street, Milsons Point, Sydney,
New South Wales 2061, Australia

RANDOM HOUSE NEW ZEALAND LTD
18 Poland Road, Glenfield, Auckland 10, New Zealand

RANDOM HOUSE (PTY) LTD
Endulini, 5A Jubilee Road, Parktown 2193, South Africa

THE RANDOM HOUSE GROUP Limited Reg. No. 954009
www.kidsatrandomhouse.co.uk

A CIP catalogue record for this book is available from the British Library.

Printed in China

Funny!

Caroline Castle & Sam Childs

HUTCHINSON

London Sydney Auckland Johannesburg

One day Little Zeb was feeling full of bounce. 'Feeling fizzy!' he told his mum. 'Feeling all springy and zingy and tip-top bubbly!'

Little Hippo was already up when Little
Zeb galloped over to the waterhole.
So they set out to find their friend
Little Piggy, who lived in the forest.

Little Zeb was so pleased to see
Little Piggy that he did a jumpy little dance:
'*Ba-doom! Ba-doom! Barangabanga-boom!*'
he sang in a deep gruff voice.

'Oh, what a funny!' cried Little Piggy and she laughed until tears ran down her snozzle.

'I'm a funny too!' cried Little Hippo.
'This is *my* dance.' Little Hippo
jumped in a muddy puddle
and wiggled his bottom from
side to side in the funniest way.
'*Ba-doom! Ba-doom!*
Badoomerooni–
boom! Boom!
BOOM!'

'That's *quite* funny,' said Little Piggy. Then she picked up two palm leaves from the forest floor and waved them about. 'But how funny is *this*?'

'Hippety-hop, hippety-hop!

Wee-wee-wee!

Ping pong!'

'Oh, very funny!' cried Little Zeb. 'Now let's all
be funny together. Copy me!'

Little Zeb began:

'Funnies to the left,
Funnies to the right,
Now wiggle your bum,
And wobble your tum!'

And Little Zeb
and Little Hippo
and Little Piggy
laughed so much
and so loudly
that they didn't
hear the rustling
of leaves and
cracking of twigs,
until . . .

BOOM!

Someone big and loud and **furious** dropped
out of the tree, *thud!* in front of them.
   '*Who* is making this terrible rumpus!' roared
the creature. 'Who are these naughties who
dare wake Big Gorilla from his sleep?'
   'Whoops-a-daisy,' said Little Zeb.

Big Gorilla swayed back and forth on his
feet in a Big Gorilla way and began to beat
his chest with his great big paws.
   The three little ones shivered with fear.

'Quick!' said
Little Zeb.
'Let's do it
again.'
   The three
friends lined
up and began:

'Funnies to the left,
Funnies to the right;
We are the funnies
And we wobble
our tummies!'

'*Ping pong!*'
finished Little Piggy.

The enormous creature
opened his eyes
very wide.

Then he quivered
and shook and
opened his great
big mouth . . .

and **roared** . . .

...with laughter!

Ha! Ha! Ha

And while he was laughing Little Zeb, Little Hippo
and Little Piggy ran away as fast as they could.
'Ooo, that was frightening!' cried Little Hippo.
'That was *scary*,' said Little Piggy.

'Yes,' said Little Zeb, 'but it was also . . .'
He wiggled his bum and wobbled his tummy.

'Tip-top funny!'

And the three friends laughed and laughed all the way home.